The Gazebo

June '08

To Hoic...
"welcome"
From,
The
Seelters'
(friends of
your grandparents
Ruettgas)

Ethel Pochocki

illustrated by
Mary Beth Owens

Mary Beth Owens

Down East Books
Camden, Maine

For Sharon Lovejoy

Mary
Francesca
Mercedes

Rosalinda
Evangeline
Yvonne

In a penthouse atop a skyscraper
in a big city, there lived a little girl named Mary Rosalinda
Francesca Evangeline Mercedes Yvonne, but her parents called
her Mary Rose. She hardly ever used her other names, except when she
visited her grandmothers and aunts, for whom she was named, or when
her teachers called on her in class.

She was a pleasant child who gave her parents much delight.
They enjoyed each other. They went to art museums and bookstores
and the ballet, and when they went out to eat, Mary Rose wore white
gloves and a velvet coat, and she always knew which fork to use.

Her life lacked for nothing,
yet there were things she wanted
and could not have–a backyard, for
one, with a garden, woods, and little
stone paths leading to the woods.
Trees with birds and bird houses,
for another.

Mary Rose wished
she could walk out the back
kitchen door and sit on the stoop,
run barefoot on dewy grass, wake on
a snowy morning and see trees covered
in sparkling white gowns. When I
grow up, she told herself, I shall
walk on grass whenever
I want.

And to this list of desires, Mary Rose added a gazebo. She had discovered gazebos one winter's day as she lay on the floor of her father's library, turning the pages of a nineteenth-century gardening book. It was large and very heavy—Mary Rose could barely lift it from the shelf. The book's leather cover was worn, and the gilt letters of the title were faded but legible:

Elegant Gardens and their Embellishments

The brittle pages cracked as she turned them, and the small, uneven print was hard to read, but the bright, glorious illustrations leaped out and carried her off easily into the landscapes of the past.

The grandmother clock gently ticked away the afternoon as Mary Rose wandered
through flower gardens and hilly orchards, mazes and manors all over the world.
She noticed that each had a tiny house, usually overlooking some lovely spot.
It was called a gazebo most of the time, but it had other names, too, beautiful
names that Mary Rose rolled around her tongue like sweet, slow-melting candy:

Belvedere - Gazebo - Kiosk - Pavilion
Glorietta
Teahouse -
Pergola
Summerhouse

Each was built according to the style
of its country, but its purpose was the same, she read. Every little house was a
set-apart place for reviewing one's gardens or estate, for entertaining or solitude,
or for "protecting oneself from the sun while outdoors without hat or umbrella."

Mary Rose studied each illustration, which fleshed out and gave life to the printed words. She saw King Amenhotep III of Egypt relaxing in his villa by the pool in 1400 B.C. She saw the summer homes of the wealthy Romans, with their pergolas facing the Mediterranean Sea.

She saw the gold-domed pavilions of Persian gardens, built
over water to keep their tiled floors cool. She saw the English
summerhouses, hidden at the center of shrubbery mazes.

Soon the sun, so bright and warm upon her when she began
to read, faded. Early twilight shadowed the room. Mary Rose
closed the book and held it to her. She did not want to leave it,
but she knew she would be coming back to it again and again,
until she knew all there was to know about gazebos.

That night, when she got into bed and closed her eyes, she could see gazebos marching past her, each inviting her in. Before she fell asleep, Mary Rose had visited Queen Victoria in her tree house in Shropshire, where they watched for foxes;

played at being milkmaids with Marie Antoinette at her hideaway at La Petite Trianon;

and shared tea with a Chinese mandarin in his pagoda. When she awoke, she was very tired from all that traveling.

In the summer, Mary Rose and her parents went
to live in their cottage on an island up north, in
Maine. Here she ran free wherever she wanted.
She hunted wildflowers in the woods,

climbed trees, and ran in the sand, her
bare feet playing tag with the waves. And
here she had her first gazebo, a birthday
gift from her parents.

It was small, just large enough for one person—two, perhaps, if they were thin. And it was simple. Slender willow and alder saplings had been skillfully woven and arched together, so that the gazebo seemed to have sprung from the earth on its own. Vines of honeysuckle and morning glory grew around the trees and made a fragrant decoration. A piece of driftwood carved with the words *Rose Cottage* hung from the opening.

Inside, there was an old tree stump for a seat and a wooden fruit crate that held a tin mug, a notebook and pencil, and whatever book Mary Rose was reading. Sometimes she sat on the stump and wrote letters to her friends in the city or wrote in her journal or just listened to the hum of bees in the honeysuckle and the wind singing through the poplars. "I could be content here forever," she thought.

She came back to the gazebo for many summers until she grew up, finished school, and chose work that would take her away from both the city and the island cottage. Mary Rose was a smart young woman with lovely manners and kind, smiling eyes, and she knew how to listen. So she became a diplomat.

Wherever the government sent her, she had a great time. It didn't matter to her where she went, for every place was new. Now she could see all the marvels of the world she had read about, and she was never disappointed. Each manor house or chateau she lived in had its own style, and to her delight, its own gazebo to match.

Sitting in each one she would think, "Oh, this is so beautiful!
This is the one I shall build someday." She kept a sketchbook of
drawings to record the details of the golden domes and copper
weather vanes and marble benches, so she would remember.

Madame Ambassador, as she was now called, became so well known that hardly a week went by without the newspapers publishing her picture launching a ship, visiting a hospital, holding a tea party for the Queen of Sweden, or single-handedly stopping a war.

Many years passed, and the dignified, silver-haired Madame Ambassador admitted to herself that she was weary of traveling. Her zest for discovery had dimmed, and besides, there was hardly a place on earth she hadn't lived. Now she wanted to begin a new chapter in her life. She wanted to write a book about her adventures. And she wanted to live in a peaceful spot where nothing happened and where she didn't have to dress up and wear pearls and a hat every day. And she wanted to sit in her own gazebo.

So she returned to the cottage on the island in Maine. It seemed
so much smaller than she remembered. The shingles were weath-
ered gray, but the windows facing the sea were unbroken and
still hung with ruffled white curtains, now limp and cobwebby.
The little cottage stood straight and sturdy but looked a bit
lonely in the midst of the wild grass and overgrown garden.

She set to work making it clean and comfortable, throwing open the windows to let in the brisk sea air. Neighbors stopped by, having seen the little curls of white smoke coming from the chimney and the laundry hanging on criss-crossed clotheslines. They called her Miss Rose and said how good it was to have her back.

When she went up to the hill, she found that the gazebo had been blown away by storms. Here and there she found pieces of the roof settling into the earth like old decayed leaves. She wondered if the *Rose Cottage* sign had been swept onto the ocean, carried off, and deposited on some distant shore for someone to find and wonder about.

"Very well," she said. "We begin again." As a diplomat Mary Rose had learned that getting upset never helped and that something good could come out of the deepest disappointment.

She sat on her rocker on the porch with her sketchbook of gazebos and went through them slowly, carefully, imagining how each would look up on the hill. None seemed right. They were either too elegant, too tall, too squat, too Oriental, or too French. None would fit in with the island's simplicity.

She closed the
sketchbook and began to
rock, refreshing her eyes with
the sight of her land framed by a
fringe of woods and stone walls. She
noticed how the willow trees reached
yearningly over into the poplars, making
an arbor over the wooden footbridge. She
saw the old plum tree, bent with age
and wind, leaning into the cherry
tree, their limbs embracing
so they seemed as one.

Miss Rose rocked and thought, and rocked and thought. Then she stopped and knew what she was going to do. The next day she ordered eight dwarf apple trees from a nursery catalog. She chose the apples with the prettiest names, savoring them as she wrote them down: Orange Cox Pippin, Winter Banana, Sheepnose, Maidenblush, Duchess of Oldenburg, Braeburn, Blue Pearmain, Sops of Wine. With such names, the apples *had* to be delicious.

By the time the trees arrived, she had dug a circle of eight deep holes in the place where the old gazebo had been, far enough apart for them to be independent but close enough to know their neighbors.

She explained to the trees that they had a mission
of great importance and asked them to please grow
strong and healthy.

Within a few years,
each tree's limbs entwined its
neighbors', like dancers in a circle.
Their topmost branches meshed into one
leafy roof, and she could no longer tell where
one tree began and another ended. In spring,
the roof was dotted with pink and white blos-
soms, like tiny ribbons on a young girl's hair.
Between and around the trunks, Miss Rose
planted climbing red roses, and the
vines wound themselves in and
out of the trees, making a
lacy lattice wall.

The floor within was cool, with smooth, thin slabs of red slate
and granite she had found in an abandoned stone wall. She
filled the spaces in between with creeping thyme. A green
rocker and a wooden table with a citronella candle and a
black-marbled notebook on it were the gazebo's furnishings.
Hanging from one of the tree limbs were wind chimes made
of bamboo. When the wind rippled through them, Miss Rose
thought they sounded like gentle waterfalls.

In September, she put on her sweater and brought a basket up to the gazebo. Inside, she reached up and picked apples of every size and color, from tiny round scarlet ones to large yellow, pink-blushed ones, from brilliant orange ones to darkly purple ones. She fondled each as a queen would her royal jewels.

The autumn sunlight dappled through the leaves onto the basket of apples and onto Miss Rose, her silver hair, and the red slate floor. In that lovely moment, breathing in the scent of apples and freshly trodden thyme, She thought, "Not even Queen Victoria or Marie Antoinette could boast a gazebo such as this."